JE NI HAO
Wait, Hoho, Wait! /
Inches, Alison.
33341007635963

Wait, Hoho, Wait!

adapted by Alison Inches
based on the screenplay written by Joe Purdy
illustrated by Daniel Mather

Ready-to-Read

SIMON SPOTLIGHT/NICKELODEON
New York   London   Toronto   Sydney

Based on the TV series *Ni Hao, Kai-lan*™ as seen on Nickelodeon®

SIMON SPOTLIGHT
An imprint of Simon & Schuster Children's Publishing Division
1230 Avenue of the Americas, New York, New York 10020
Manufactured in the United States of America
10 9
Library of Congress Cataloging-in-Publication Data
Inches, Alison.
Wait, Hoho, wait! / adapted by Alison Inches ; from a teleplay by Joe
Purdy. — 1st ed.
p. cm. — (Ready-to-read)
"Based on the TV series Ni Hao Kai-lan as seen on Nick Jr."— Copyright
page.
ISBN 978-1-4169-8519-8
0610 LAK
I. Purdy, Joe. II. Ni Hao Kai-lan (Television program) III. Title.
PZ7.I355Wai 2009
[E — dc22
2008050143

Ni hao! I'm 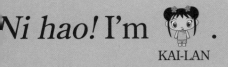.

KAI-LAN

Today 🐯 got a new toy 🚗!

RINTOO   CAR

🐵 wants to ride in the 🚗 right now.

HOHO   CAR

Not yet, .

HOHO

 and  have to

RINTOO   TOLEE

build the  first.

CAR

The  has lots of parts.
CAR

It will take some time.

watches  and  .

HOHO   RINTOO   TOLEE

They put the  parts

CAR

on the ground.

They have , a , ,

DOORS   STEERING WHEEL   HEADLIGHTS

, and a .

WHEELS   MIRROR

"Is the  ready yet?" asks .

CAR   HOHO

"Not yet!" say  and .

RINTOO   TOLEE

 really wants to ride

HOHO

in the toy .

CAR

He stomps his feet and hops up

and down.

Then he jumps in the toy .

CAR

Crash!

The falls apart.

CAR

Oh, no!

did not know how to wait.

HOHO

 and  will have to start over.

RINTOO   TOLEE

 is very sorry.

HOHO

How can  learn how to wait?
HOHO

Hey, look at  .
YEYE

When he has to wait, he does

something he likes. He sings.

know! If  does something he HOHO

kes, waiting will be easier!

When waiting is hard for you,

o something you like to do!

What does  like to do? HOHO

 likes to play "Where's ?"
HOHO   HOHO

Is  in the 🏠?
   HOHO   SHED

No!

Is  in the ⬤ patch?

HOHO   PUMPKIN

No!

Is  in the ?
HOHO   TREE
Yes!

We found !
                    HOHO

"Is the  ready yet?" asks 🐵.

CAR   HOHO

"Not yet," say 🐯 and 🐨.

RINTOO   TOLEE

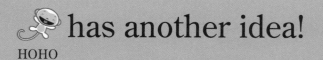 has another idea!

HOHO

He will build a rock tower.

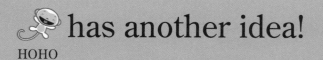 is doing a good job waiting.

HOHO

"Is the  ready yet?" asks .
CAR HOHO

"Not yet!" say and .
RINTOO TOLEE

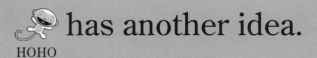 has another idea.
HOHO

He plays music on his  .

TURNTABLES

"Is the  ready?" asks .
CAR   HOHO

"Yes! The  is done!"
CAR

say  and .
RINTOO   TOLEE

Wow!  did a super job waiting.
HOHO

Now all we need is a push.

Can you help us?

Say "Push!"

Here we go!

What a super 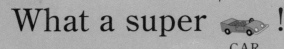 !
CAR

Thanks for helping  learn
HOHO

how to wait.

You make my ♥ feel super happy
HEART

ELIJAH